This Book Belongs To:

Radiant

Nicole M. Allen

Illustrations by Josie Yee

Rainbow

ISBN 13: 978-0-9980424-0-4

Cover Design: Glen Edelstein, Hudson Valley Book Design
Book Design: Glen Edelstein, Hudson Valley Book Design
Illustrations: Josie Yee
Author photo: Nick Carter

Printed in the United States of America

To my husband, my boys, family, and friends who have supported and encouraged my dreams; and to the next generation of girl scientists and engineers who will amplify the beauty and magic of science.

Scilie G. Powers sat in her bedroom filled with all the things she adored. She loved her soft bed, fluffy rug, pretty curtains, and her fancy tutu-wearing doll collection. Scilie also loved the artwork and posters on her walls that inspired her to be her best and explore her world. Her bedroom made her happy, but outside, it was a dark and gloomy day.

"I just want the rain to stop!" she said. Since the early morning hours, the rain had poured down from the gray clouds in the sky. Scilie heard loud claps of thunder and saw bolts of lightning in the distance.

She imagined all the amazing things she would do outside if it were not raining. Scilie thought about picking sunflowers, playing at the park with her friends, riding her bike, or dancing through the neighborhood, but the rain continued.

As Scilie looked for something to explore, her eyes stopped at her doll collection. The dolls sat on a shelf across from her bed. Even her dolls' smiles were upside down today, except for one doll. Her red doll was smiling.

I wonder why she is so happy? Scilie thought, but she continued with her day.

Her mother suggested activities that Scilie and her little sister, Matilyn, could do together.

They played games, read books, and did science experiments.

After a fun morning, the afternoon brought something wonderful!

The rain had finally stopped, the sun was starting to shine, and Scilie began to smile. Her grin was so big because she saw something radiant appear in the distance.

"A rainbow!" she shouted. It was clear as could be, up high in the sky next to the clouds.

Scilie was so excited to see the rainbow and was even more excited that it was time to play outside! Now, she was very happy, and so were all her dolls! She noticed all of them were smiling.

How does this pretty thing appear?
she thought.

What makes it show in front of my eyes up high
next to the clouds in the sky?

It must have something to do with the rain or the sun or the
clouds, she said to herself.

I need to find out what makes a radiant rainbow appear! Scilie knew what to do when she had a question and needed direction. She looked at her doll collection. "Hmm . . .," she said, "which one of you will help me today?"

In her closet, hidden under a huge pile of sandals, ballet flats, flip-flops, dress shoes, and sneakers, Scilie found a shoebox. Nestled in that box was a case that lit up when she opened it. Scilie squealed with delight, as she knew this was where she would find the answer!

Slowly, she pulled out the most beautiful pair of glasses decorated with her name and glitter and purple, pink, orange, and yellow stones. These were not just ordinary glasses. These were magic safety glasses! Scilie knew that when she explored something, the very first step was to protect herself.

She heard magical sounds and saw sparkle and glitter fill the room as she placed the glasses on her face.

Suddenly, Scilie saw a new exciting place! She was walking and turning and spinning around until she found her red tutu-wearing doll!

"Hi, I'm Phyllis. Welcome to my rainbow lab. I'm a physicist. I will show you how that radiant rainbow appeared."

"You're a what?" asked Scilie.

"I'm a physicist. Follow me," said Phyllis. "You asked the question, made a guess, and now it's time to find out why!"

Scilie followed her life-sized doll through an amazing rainbow playland. She climbed into the empty swing next to Matilyn, ready to learn a new lesson.

Phyllis said, "All the answers can be found in one word, and that word is science! It tells us how things happen. It's all around! It's everywhere! Science, Scilie, is in all the rainbows out there!"

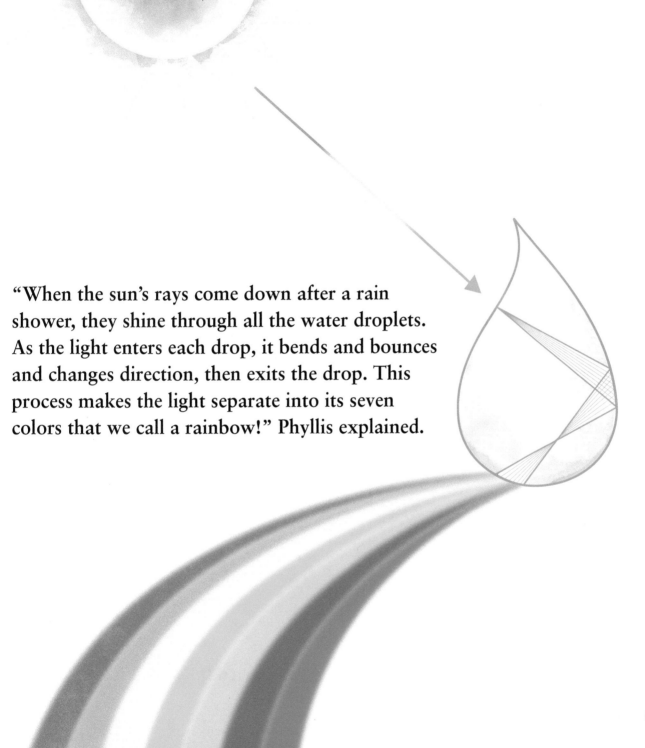

"When the sun's rays come down after a rain shower, they shine through all the water droplets. As the light enters each drop, it bends and bounces and changes direction, then exits the drop. This process makes the light separate into its seven colors that we call a rainbow!" Phyllis explained.

R O Y **G** B **I V**

Red
  Orange

    Green
      Blue
        Indigo
          Violet

Phyllis said, "Think of the colors as your friend, Roy G. Biv."

"Let's experiment: What do you think will happen when we shine light through this glass of water?" asked Phyllis.

Scilie thought for a moment and wrote the guess, called a hypothesis, on her paper and said, "I think we will see something amazing! Will the light bend like it does in the raindrops?"

"You are right," Phyllis said. "The light is bending, bouncing, and changing direction in the glass of water until you see a rainbow on the paper! When you see a rainbow anywhere, light has separated into its seven colors! I study how light moves and separates and lots of other things that help people understand why certain things happen that seem magical, like a rainbow," explained Phyllis.

Scilie understood now why Phyllis was smiling this morning.
"You knew that I might see a rainbow after the rain stopped
and knew I would want to find out how it happens!"
exclaimed Scilie.

"This part of science is called physics. You have the power
to be a physicist one day, too, or anything you want to be!"
Phyllis said.

"My parents always tell me to remember my name, Scilie G.
Powers. The G. is for girl. Girl Powers!" she exclaimed.

Phyllis said all the answers can be found in one big word, and that word is science.

It's everywhere!

Science, science everywhere!

Science is in all the rainbows out there!

Scilie slowly took her glasses off and let her eyes adjust. "Wow!" she said. "That was a great lesson!"

At the park, she told her friends how rainbows are made.

Scilie loves rainbows even more now.

Now she knows rainbows are science.

She wants to wear them all the time on her shirts, socks, and on her ears.
She wants to wear them all the time on her purse, bracelets, and in her hair!

Science, science everywhere!

Science is in all the rainbows out there!

About the Author

 Nicole M. Allen earned Bachelor of Science degrees in Computer Science and Electrical Engineering from Spelman College and the Georgia Institute of Technology, respectively, before working at power utility companies while attaining a Master of Engineering degree from Vanderbilt University. She saw, first-hand, the need to encourage more girls to study science and engineering disciplines as one of only a few women in classes and the workplace. In her début book series, Nicole hopes to introduce the glitz and glam of science to children and increase the number of female scientists and engineers. Nicole lives in New York with her husband, two boys, and their endless supply of science books, games, and experiments.

About the Illustrator

 Josie Yee is an award-winning illustrator and graphic artist specializing in children's publishing. She has illustrated over a hundred traditional mass market and trade books during her extensive career. She is published with many major publishers including Random House, Scholastic Inc., and Disney Press. Josie received her Bachelor of Fine Arts degree from Arizona State University and later went on to study Illustration at the Academy of Art University in San Francisco, California and the School of Visual Arts in New York City. Josie works and plays in New York City.

THIS BOOK BELONGS TO:

Best friends come in all shapes and sizes.
Your new best friend is waiting for you.

I'M A SECRET SUPERHERO

To Hales Corners Elementary—Think positive thoughts! :)

Marla McKenna

Written by Marla McKenna

Illustrations by Brenda Kato

Quantity order requests can be emailed to:
publishing@rejilaberje.com

Or mailed to:
Reji Laberje Writing and Publishing
Publishing Orders
234 W. Broadway Street
Waukesha, WI 53186

Author: Marla McKenna
I'm a Secret Superhero

Illustrations, Cover & Interior Layout: Brenda Kato
Visit brendakato.com
Author Photo by Julia McKenna

ISBN-10: 194590710X
ISBN-13: 978-1945907104

SALES Categories:
Children's Books | Growing Up & Facts of Life | Friendship, Social Skills & School Life | Self-Esteem & Self-Respect
Children's Books | Comics & Graphic Novels | Superheroes
Children's Books | Early Learning | Beginner Readers

BISAC Codes:
JUV008080 JUVENILE FICTION | Comics & Graphic Novels | Fantasy
JUV039140 JUVENILE FICTION | Social Themes | Self-Esteem & Self-Reliance
EDU023000 EDUCATION | Early Childhood

www.rejilaberje.com

Reji Laberje

Writing and Publishing

Dedication From Marla

To God, He works all things together for good.

To my beautiful daughters, Ashley and Julia, with love.

Dedication From Brenda

To my three great nieces: Baleigh, Peyton and Tatum. I thank Marla for giving me this opportunity to illustrate her children's book. I thank God for my talents, my senses and this life experience. Thanks to my inner circle of family and friends for their support during my never ending creative projects: my parents Angie & Dean, my two sisters, Deanne and Rhonda, my sweet nieces, Sarah, Madeleine, Deleah and Kara, my nephews, Robert, Steven, Lee, Will, Christian, my man Jason and my faithful dogs. Thanks to Core Love for developing the g.life energy healing technology I need to heal my body. Thanks to "The Secret" for teaching me how to manifest my dreams.

Flying by the moon I see
its bright light shining over me.
The beams they shimmer with the stars
and guide my way to where you are.

The Universe is grand and full of power
and sends out happiness like a meteor shower.
It gives out love for me to share
so others can feel how much I care.

Positive thoughts, they make me smile
and I feel stronger all the while.
For there's no room for negative, can't you see?
Thinking happy thoughts is the only way for me.

And when I give back, that's always the best.
But sometimes it can sure put us to the test.
Trusting my heart is how I will know,
which is the direction for me to go.

As the night sky disappears and turns on the sun
its radiance dances until the day is once again done.
But during that time, I have choices to make,
yes, I can choose kindness for goodness sake.

Being a great friend, is what I will be
for friendships, they are important to me.
I won't gossip, judge or hurt with my actions
and this will bring me much satisfaction.

My light within is what shines through.
It glows brighter and brighter in everything that I do.
For being beautiful inside is what matters to me.
That's really important, don't you agree?

And I will be thankful I am in this life here
with all that I have, I will show good cheer.
Being grateful is the key that unlocks my dreams,
this I know for sure, and so it seems.

For sunflowers and daisies and butterflies of blue
this wonderful life, it can happen for you.
For sunshine and raindrops and thunderstorms too,
in all of its beauty, it teaches us to be true.

True to ourselves, it's the gift we've been given,
to live our life's purpose for which we have risen.
The Universe, in all its splendor, gives us signs if we listen.
It's the music only we can hear that makes our souls glisten.

Flying high in the sky or standing my ground,
I always know where my answers can be found.
For the powers I have are not super at all,
they are the positive thoughts that I think,
they make me stand tall!

Donations:

The mission of the Linda Blair WorldHeart Foundation is to make sure that every animal they rescue is given a second chance at a happy life and a loving forever home. Thank you to all those involved in making this wonderful Foundation possible. Partial proceeds from this book are donated to their cause, with special thanks to Rick Springfield and his family for their generosity in matching this donation. Every dog deserves to be loved, and together we can all make that happen.
Thank you for your support!